For David

VIKING

Published by the Penguin Group

Penguin Putnam Books for Young Readers, 345 Hudson Street, New York, New York 10014, U.S.A.

Penguin Books Ltd, 27 Wrights Lane, London W8 5TZ, England

Penguin Books Australia Ltd, Ringwood, Victoria, Australia

Penguin Books Canada Ltd, 10 Alcorn Avenue, Toronto, Ontario, Canada M4V 3B2

Penguin Books (N.Z.) Ltd, 182-190 Wairau Road, Auckland 10, New Zealand

Penguin Books Ltd, Registered Offices: Harmondsworth, Middlesex, England

First published in 1970 by The Macmillan Company

Published in 1999 by Viking, a member of Penguin Putnam Books for Young Readers

12

LIBRARY OF CONGRESS CATALOGING-IN-PUBLICATION DATA
Keats, Ezra Jack.
Hi, cat! / Ezra Jack Keats. p. cm.
Summary: Archie's day would have been great if he had not started
it by greeting the new cat on the block.
ISBN 978-0-670-88546-6 (hardcover)
[1. Cats—Fiction. 2. Afro-Americans—Fiction.] I. Title.
PZ7.K2253Hi 1999 [E]—dc21 98-37764 CIP AC

Manufactured in China
Set in Bembo

HI, CAT!

EZRA JACK KEATS

VIKING

On his way to meet Peter,
Archie saw someone new on the block.

"Hi, cat," he said as he walked by.

He looked at his reflection in a store window.

Peter was waiting at the corner.
"Make way for your ol' gran'pa,"
Archie said in a shaky voice.
He looked Peter up and down.
"My, my, Peter, how you've grown!"

"Why, gran'pa," Peter said.
"It's good to see you."
"Hello, my children," Archie croaked.
"Hi, gran'pa!" Susy giggled.

Willie was so happy to see Archie
he ran over and licked his face.
Archie tasted delicious!
Willie licked and licked and licked.

"No respect for old age!"

Archie whispered something to Peter and ran off.
"Stick around, folks," Peter called.
"We have a surprise for you."

When Archie got back,
he and Peter worked
while everyone waited.

"OK!" Peter announced.
"Make way for Mister Big Face!"
A big paper bag appeared.
Then a tongue stuck out of one of the eyes!

A hand came out of an ear
and motioned everyone to move closer.
They all obeyed.

Suddenly the bag began to shake.

It shook harder, and harder, and —

MEEOOW!

People started to leave.

"Wait—wait—the show'll go on!
See the tallest dog in the world
take a walk!" Archie shouted.

"Some show, gran'pa!"
"Some tall dog!"
"Who ate your mustache, gran'pa?"
Everyone walked away, laughing.
Soon no one was left except Archie, Peter,
Willie and the torn paper bag.

"It would have been great
   if it wasn't for that crazy cat," said Peter
   as they walked home.
"Mmmm," said Archie. "He sure stuck around."

"...and all I said was 'Hi, cat,'" said Archie,
  finishing his story.
"You're well rid of a cat like that,"
  said his mother.
  Archie thought for a while.
"You know what, Ma?" he said.
"I think that cat just kinda liked me!"